Just A Gingerbread Man

Written by:

Alyssa Wilburn

Illustrated by:

Tabitha Hamm

To order additional copies of this book, contact:
Xlibris
844-714-8691
www.Xlibris.com
Orders@Xlibris.com

ISBN: Softcover   978-1-6698-1383-5
       EBook   978-1-6698-1382-8

Print information available on the last page

Rev. date: 03/02/2022

Just A

Gingerbread Man

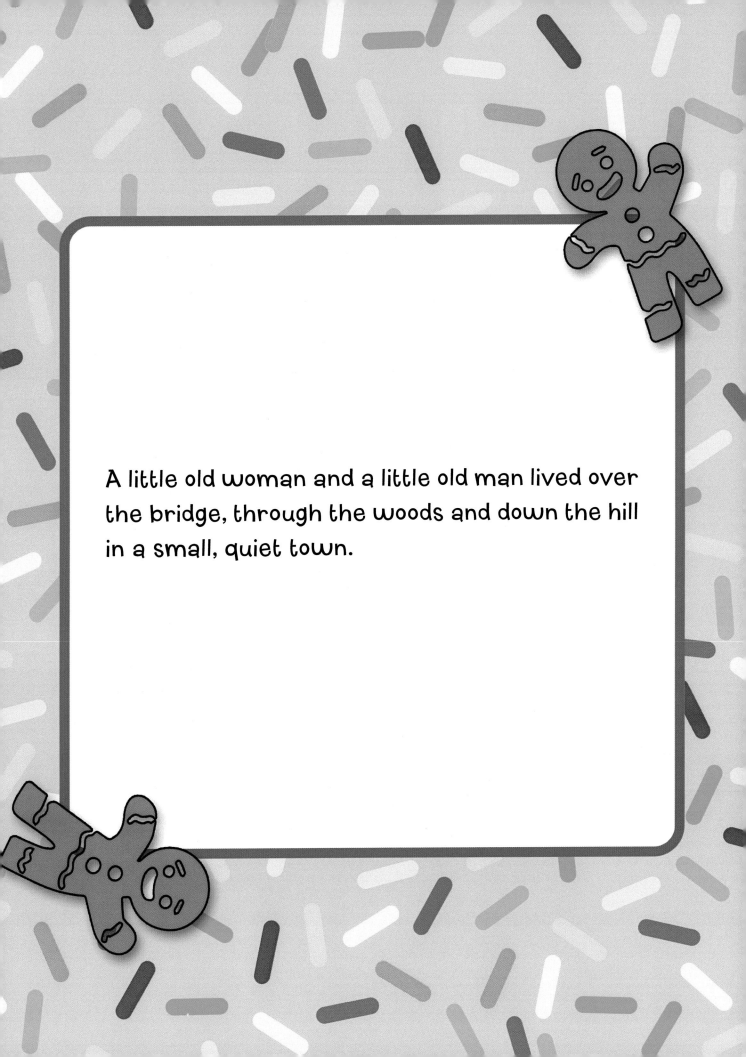

A little old woman and a little old man lived over the bridge, through the woods and down the hill in a small, quiet town.

They lived in a little house all alone and they were very grumpy.

Nothing was ever right. Their house was too small. Their garden never grew..

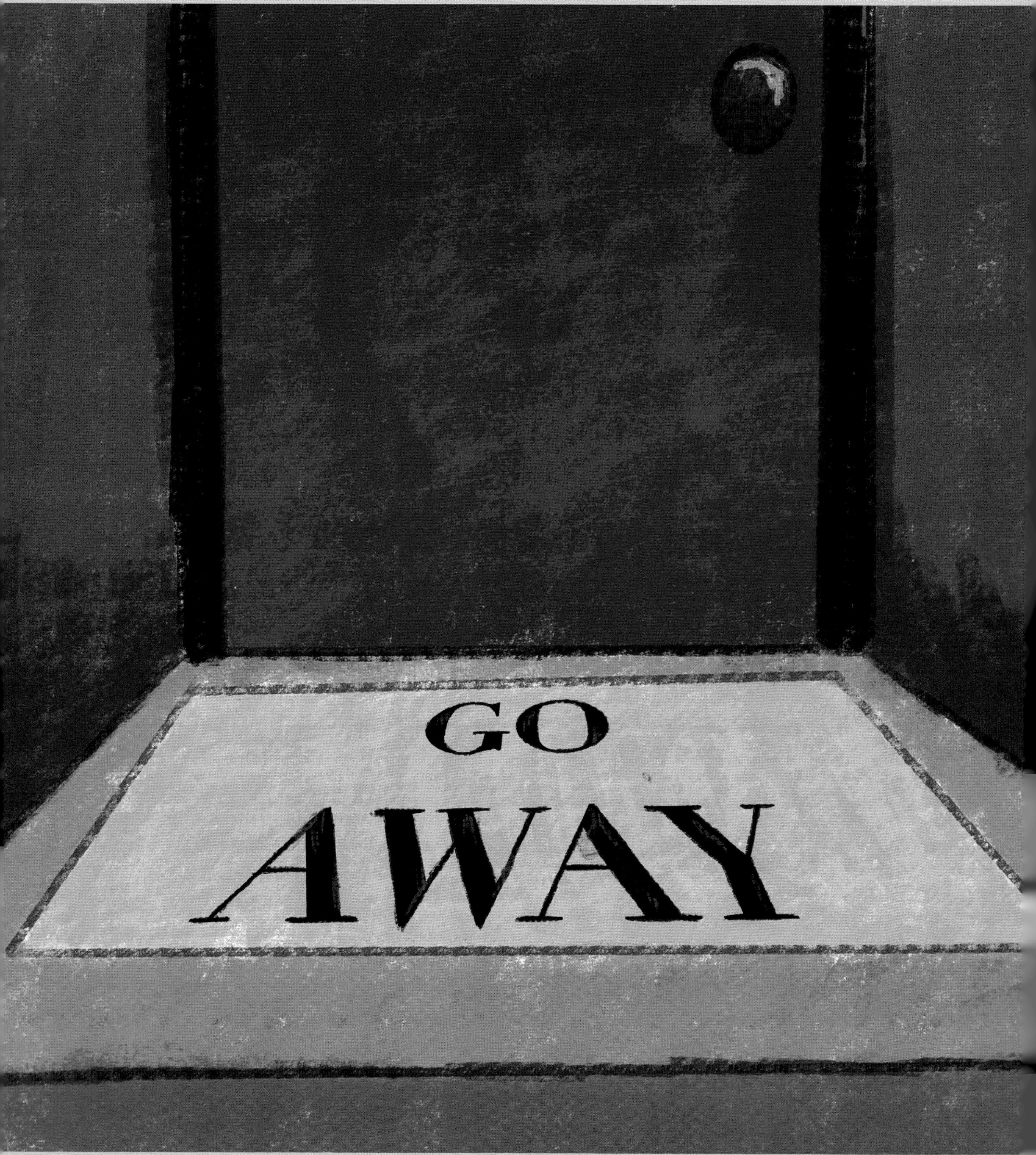
GO
AWAY

They did not like visitors or have friends over for dinner.

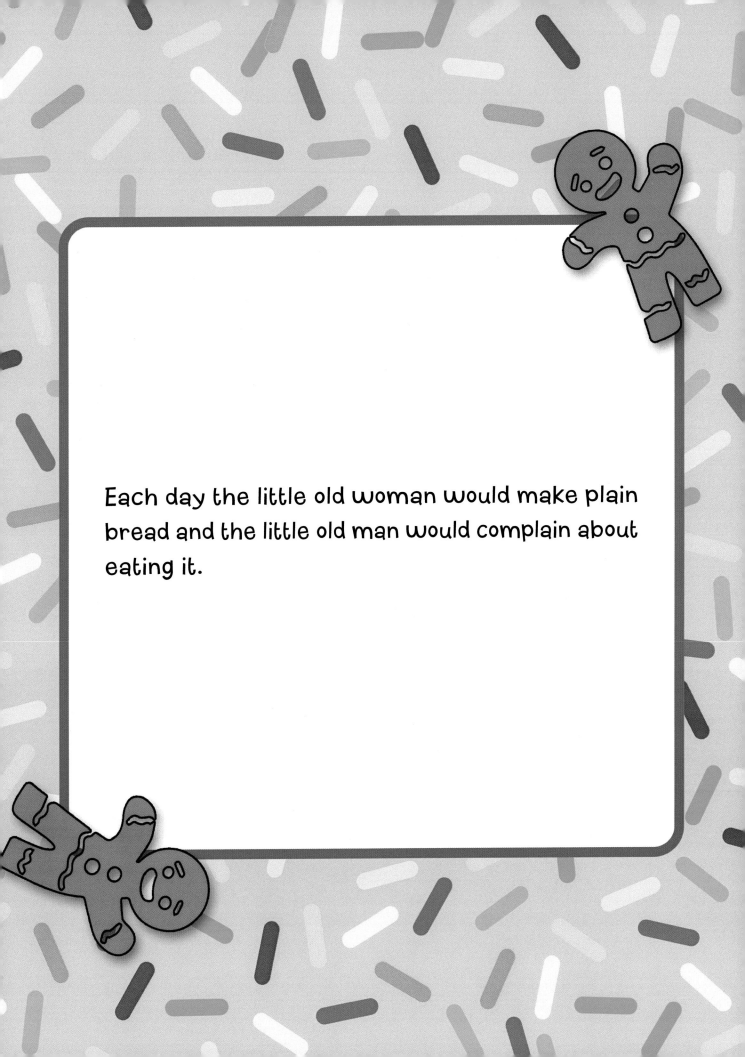

Each day the little old woman would make plain bread and the little old man would complain about eating it.

"Why can't you make something better. I want something sweet." He would say to her as they ate their plain bread and salad, a salad that was also plain and too small.

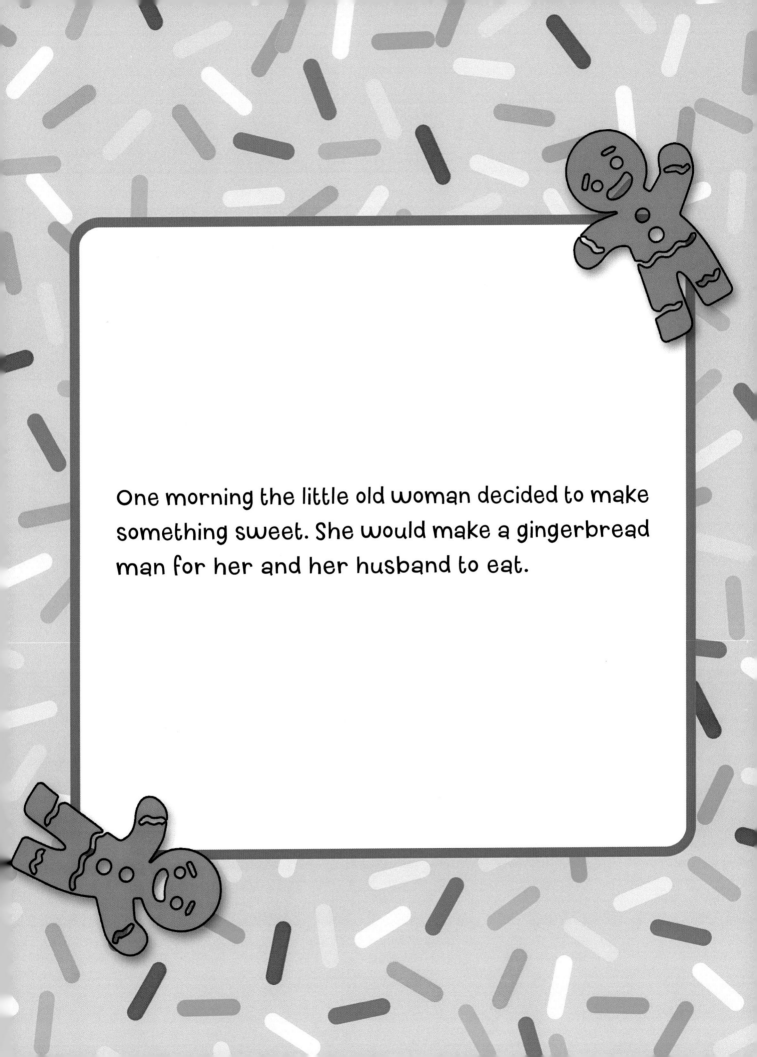

One morning the little old woman decided to make something sweet. She would make a gingerbread man for her and her husband to eat.

He would be just the right size for a tasty treat for them to share. There would be nothing left once they ate him up!

The little old woman rolled out the dough. She cut the dough into the shape of a gingerbread man. She added three bright red candy buttons and some pants made with icing. She popped him in the oven and cleaned the dishes while she waited for him to bake.

The little old man came into the house and smelled the sweet scent of cinnamon and sugar. "What is that smell? I've never smelt anything like it in this house. What did you do?". The little old woman was very proud of her work and explained that she had made a tasty snack for them to eat if the little old man could be patient and wait for it to finish baking.

In the oven, something more than baking was happening. The gingerbread man was coming alive! He could hear the grumpy people outside the oven talking about eating him. Why would they want to eat a gingerbread man? The gingerbread man was scared.

He didn't want to be a tasty snack to anyone. He needed an escape plan, and quick. He looked through the window in the oven and saw the window by the front door was open. "I'll run out and jump through the window!" He said to himself. "They'll never catch me."

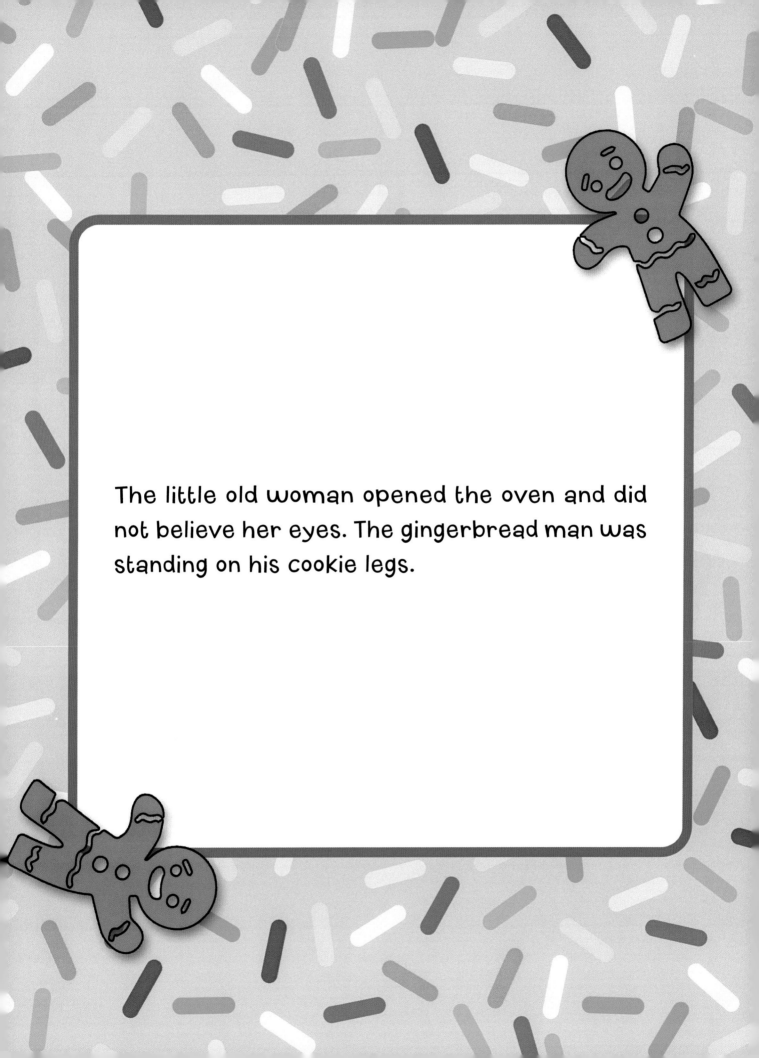

The little old woman opened the oven and did not believe her eyes. The gingerbread man was standing on his cookie legs.

Before she could blink he had hopped down from the oven and out the window. She turned to her husband. He was as wide-eyed and surprised as she was. Before they could say a word they were both running to the front door.

The little old woman started to call after the gingerbread man, "Come back here gingerbread man! You are supposed to be our tasty snack." The gingerbread man didn't slow down.

He turned and saw the little old woman and the little old man hot on his trail.

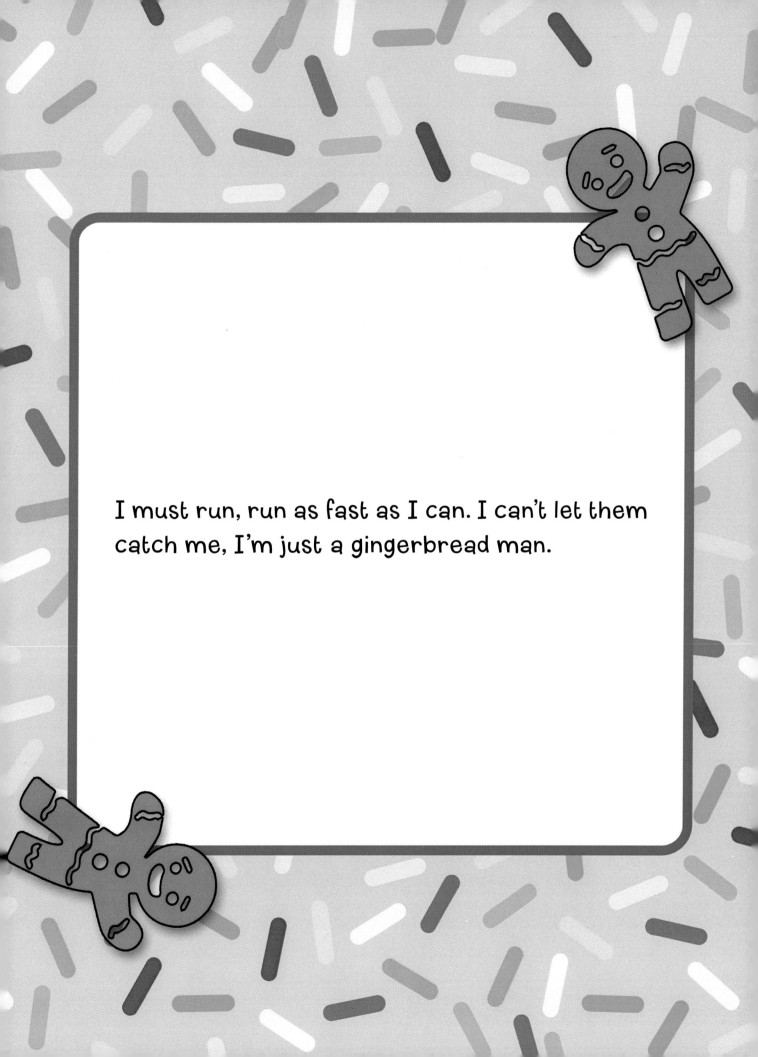

I must run, run as fast as I can. I can't let them catch me, I'm just a gingerbread man.

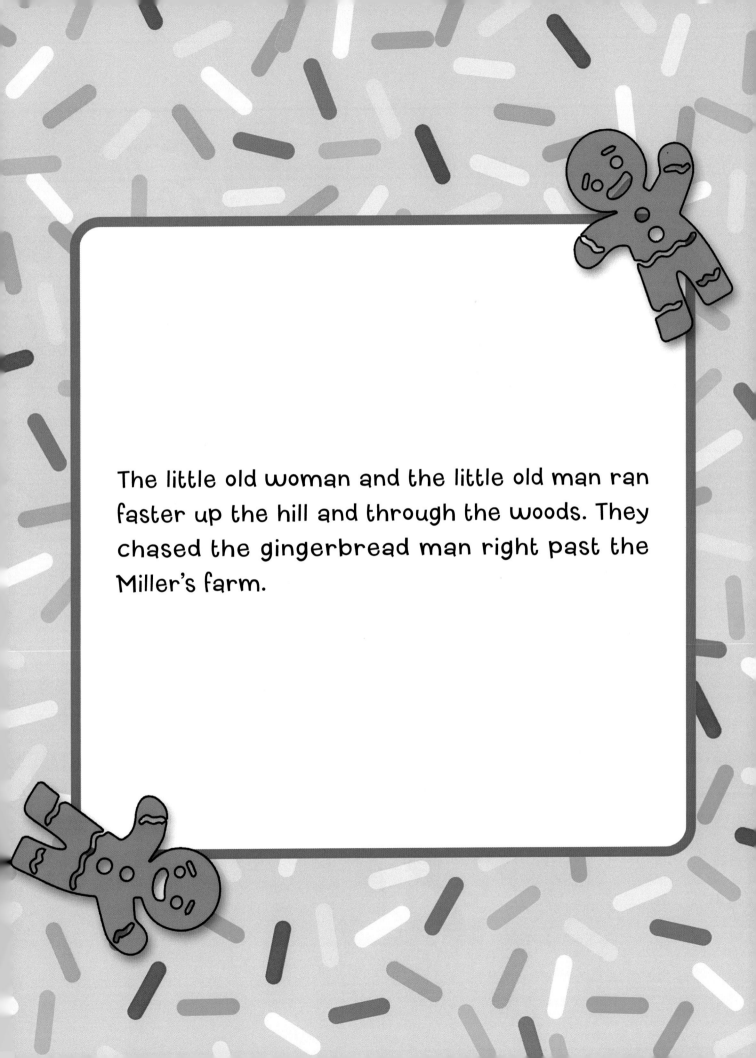

The little old woman and the little old man ran faster up the hill and through the woods. They chased the gingerbread man right past the Miller's farm.

A herd of cows were enjoying the cool breeze, blowing the grass around their hooves.

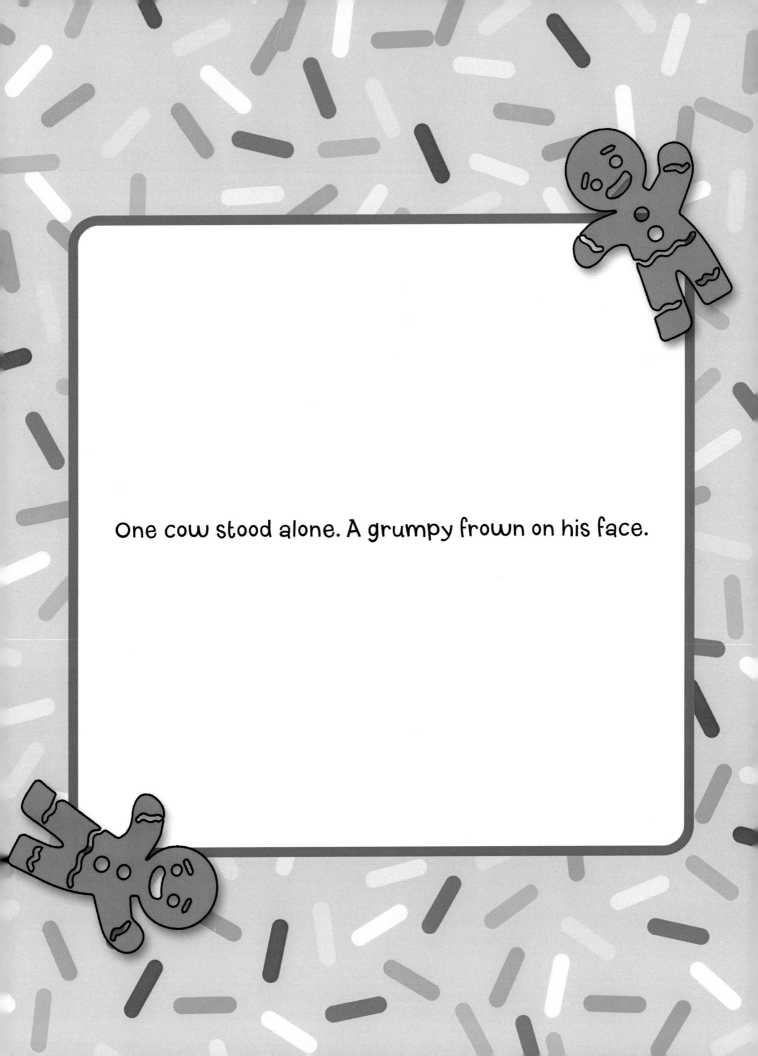

One cow stood alone. A grumpy frown on his face.

He spotted the gingerbread man and the little old woman and the little old man running to the woods. The smell of gingerbread tickled his nose and he too joined the chase. The cow started to call after the gingerbread man, "Come back here gingerbread man! You smell like a tasty snack." The gingerbread man didn't slow down. He turned and saw the grumpy cow hot on his trail too.

I must run, run as fast as I can. I can't let them catch me, I'm just a gingerbread man.

The little old woman and the little old man and the cow ran faster up the hill and through the woods and past the Miller's farm. They chased the gingerbread man right past the Miller's pond.

A gaggle of geese were swimming, looking for breadcrumbs to munch on.

One goose swam alone. A grumpy frown on his face.

He spotted the gingerbread man and the little old woman and the little old man running to the woods. The shiny red candy buttons on the gingerbread man caught his attention. They looked delicious and he joined the chase too.

The goose started to call after the gingerbread man, "Come back here gingerbread man! You look like a tasty snack." The gingerbread man didn't slow down. He turned and saw the grumpy goose hot on his trail too.

I must run, run as fast as I can. I can't let them catch me, I'm just a gingerbread man.

The little old woman and the little old man and the cow ran faster up the hill and through the woods and past the Miller's farm and past the Miller's pond. The gingerbread man came to a river. There was nowhere else to run.

A sleeping fox nearby woke from all the noise of the little old woman and the little old man and the cow and the goose yelling and chasing after the gingerbread man. The fox approached the gingerbread man with a sweet and gentle smile.

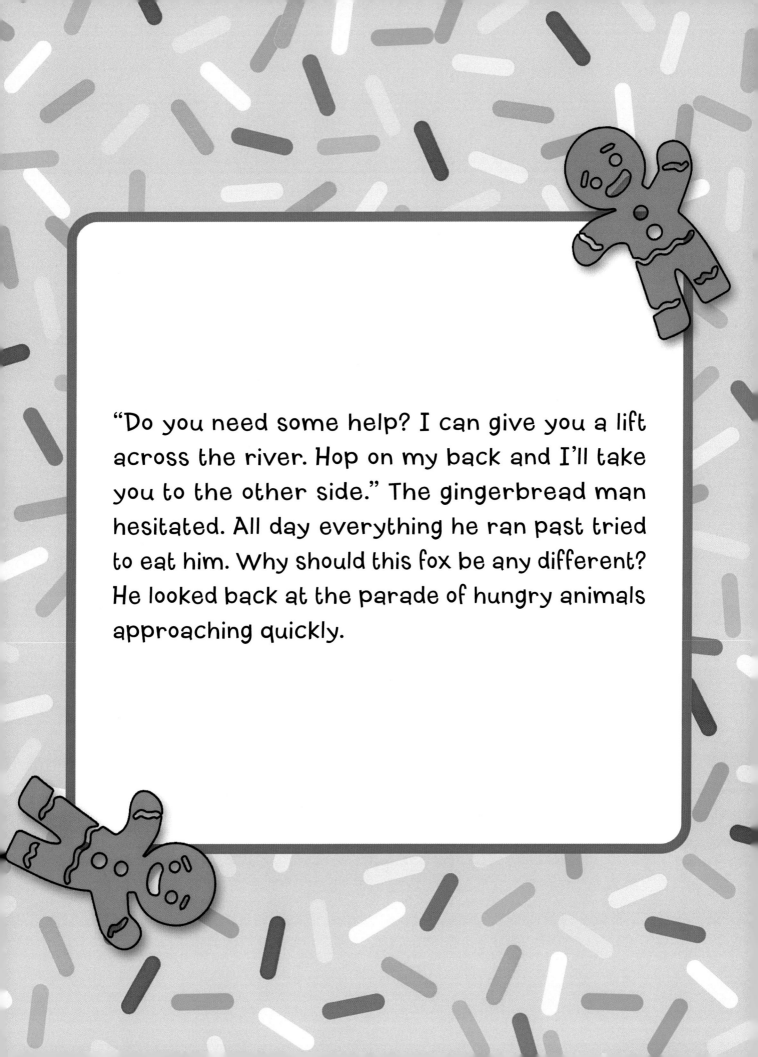

"Do you need some help? I can give you a lift across the river. Hop on my back and I'll take you to the other side." The gingerbread man hesitated. All day everything he ran past tried to eat him. Why should this fox be any different? He looked back at the parade of hungry animals approaching quickly.

He hopped on the fox's back and she swiftly dove into the water. They were halfway across. The fox said, "move up to head. The water is getting deeper and you'll get soggy." WIthout hesitation this time, the gingerbread man moved up to the fox's head.

The little old woman and the little old man and the cow and the goose were all standing at the edge of the river. They had grumpy frowns on their faces as they watched the fox deliver the gingerbread man safely across the river, and out of their reach.

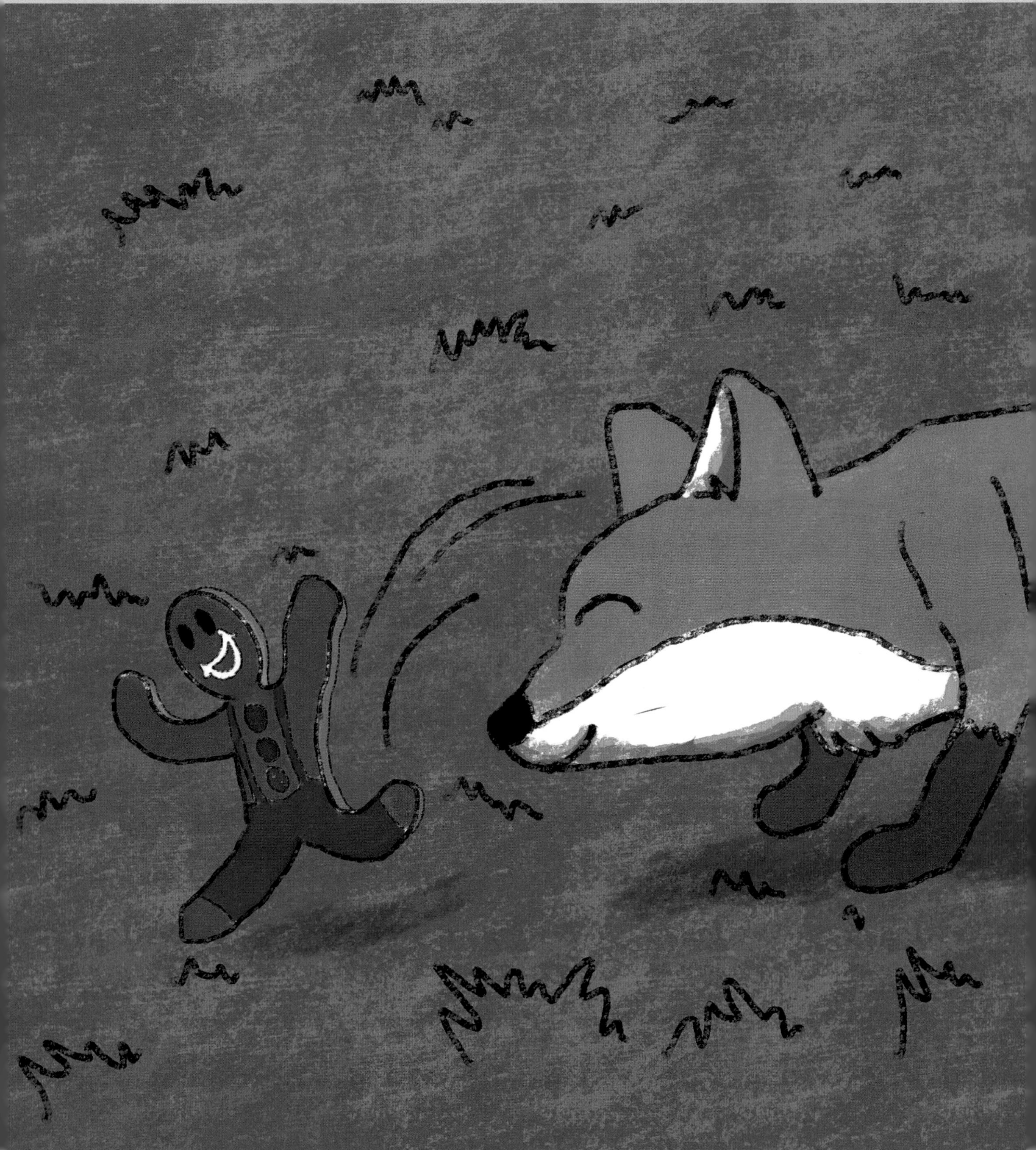

With a quick flip off the fox's head and a bow, the gingerbread man and his new friend, Miss fox, walked away and lived happily ever after.

The End

Printed in the United States
by Baker & Taylor Publisher Services